For the latest crop of little monkeys: Christina, Elin, and Starlin

Clarion Books
215 Park Avenue South
New York, New York 10003

Clarion Books is an imprint of Houghton Mifflin Harcourt Publishing Company.

www.hmhbooks.com

The illustrations were executed digitally in pen and ink with color.
The text was set in 18-point Cantoria.
Cookie recipe on back endpaper courtesy of Tracey Campbell Pearson

Library of Congress Cataloging-in-Publication Data
Christelow, Eileen.
Five little monkeys trick-or-treat / Eileen Christelow.
p. cm.
Summary: When babysitter Lulu takes the five little monkeys trick-or-treating, they decide to
change costumes with their friends and try to fool Lulu and their mother.
ISBN 978-0-547-85893-7 (hardcover)
[1. Halloween—Fiction. 2. Costume—Fiction. 3. Monkeys—Fiction.
4. Behavior—Fiction. 5. Babysitters—Fiction.] I. Title.
PZ7.C4523Fk 2013
[E]—dc23
2012025208

Manufactured in China
SCP 10 9 8 7 6 5 4 3 2 1
4500411619

FIVE Little MONKEYS
trick-or-treat

Eileen Christelow

CLARION BOOKS

Houghton Mifflin Harcourt ● Boston   New York   2013

THE five little monkeys dress up for Halloween. "Hurry!" says Mama. "Your favorite babysitter is here to take you trick-or-treating."

Costume Stuff

3

"Hi, Lulu!" shout the monkeys. "Banana, alien, ghost, goblin, and princess are ready to go!"

"But I was going out with the five little monkeys!" says Lulu. "Where are they?"

"They're taking a nap," giggles the princess.

5

Off they go.

"Ghost, princess, goblin, banana, and alien," Mama reminds Lulu. "Don't lose the rascals!"

"Don't worry!" says Lulu.

Down the street, the alien meets a friend.

"Nice bunny costume!" says the alien.

"I like yours better!" says the friend.

"We could trade," suggests the alien.

"Everyone will be SO confused!" they whisper.

As the other trick-or-treaters run down the street,
Lulu checks: "Banana, ghost, goblin, princess . . .
Uh-oh! WHERE IS THE ALIEN?"

"Here he comes!" exclaims the princess.
"Now, look here, Mr. Alien," Lulu scolds.
"You monkeys need to stick with me!"

"That is the best Halloween trick ever!" whispers the ghost. "I wish I could switch costumes!" The banana spies two more trick-or-treater friends.

It turns out the television would love to switch costumes.
"I'd much rather be a big yellow banana!" she says.

The ghost and the robot switch costumes too.
"This is SO funny!" they squeal. "Lulu will never notice!"

The ghost and the banana catch up just as Lulu is checking again: "Alien, princess, goblin . . . whew! Ghost, banana!"

14

"Everyone is switching costumes!"
giggles the goblin. "This is so silly!"
"We could switch costumes too!"
suggest two more trick-or-treater friends.

"Good idea!" says the goblin. "This is the best Halloween trick!"
"Pleased to help," says the pumpkin.

The grapes and the princess decide to trade too.
"Lulu won't even notice!" says the princess.

When the goblin and the princess catch up,
Lulu doesn't SEEM to notice a thing.
"You monkeys are just in time!" she tells them.

Then Lulu counts, "Princess, goblin, ghost, alien, banana . . . Oh, good. I have all five little monkeys!"

The other trick-or-treaters think THAT is hilarious!

21

But then Lulu hustles the princess, banana, goblin, ghost, and alien down the street.

"See you around!" she calls to the other trick-or-treaters. "We have to get home for a big Halloween treat!"

"Uh-oh!" cries the big blue bunny.

Lulu delivers the banana, ghost, alien, princess, and goblin home to Mama.
"I didn't lose one!" she says.

24

Mama gasps. "They look different!"
"Oh, don't worry about THAT!" says Lulu.
And then the doorbell rings . . .

"Trick-or-treat, Mama!"
Mama looks very carefully at the trick-or-treaters.

"There must be some mistake," she says. "Because I am the mama of a banana, alien, ghost, princess, and goblin. And they are already home."

Mama closes the door . . . almost.
"Uh-oh!"

But then she peeks out.

"Why don't you rascals come in for a treat?"

29

Mama hugs her monkeys, then scolds them. "Poor Lulu! This is trick-OR-treat, not trick-AND-treat!"

"That's okay," says Lulu. "I've made the perfect treat for tricksters!"

33

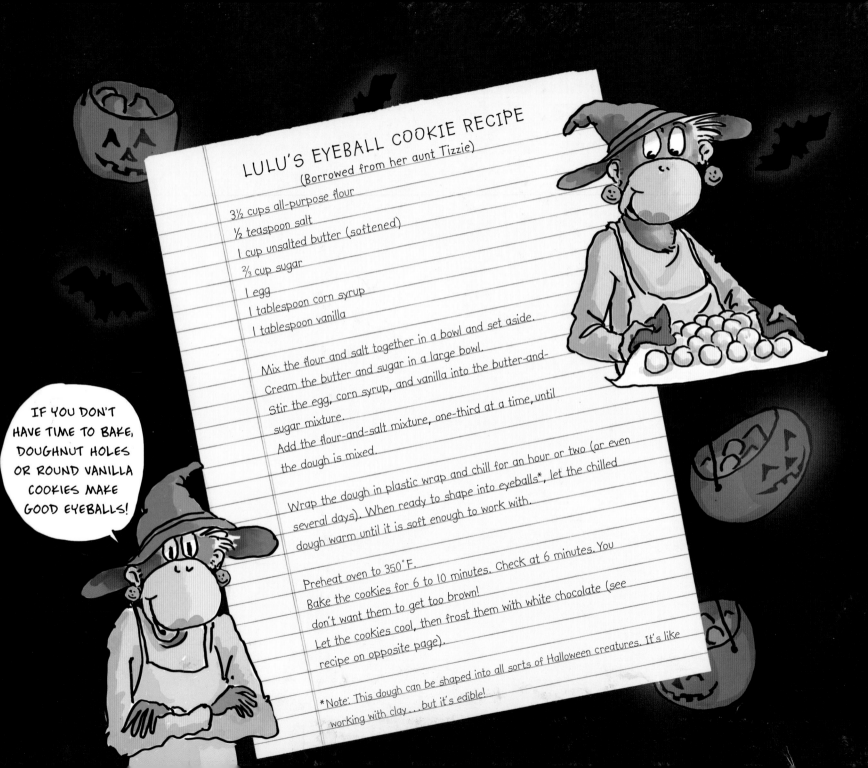